Secret PRINCESSES

Seaside Fun

ROSIE BANKS

Wishing Star Palace

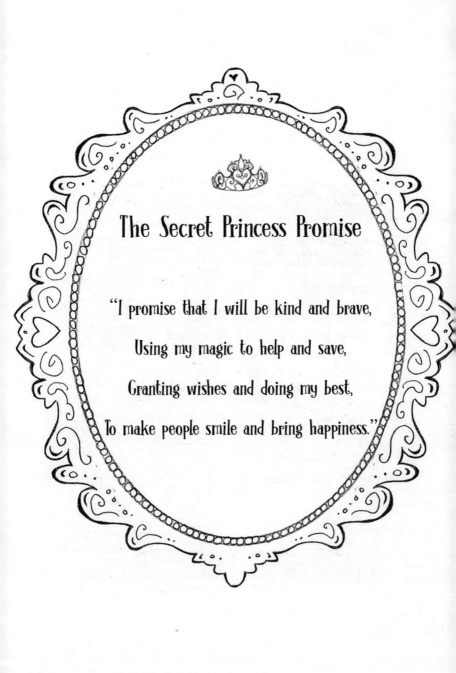

The Secret Princess Promise

"I promise that I will be kind and brave,

Using my magic to help and save,

Granting wishes and doing my best,

To make people smile and bring happiness."

CONTENTS

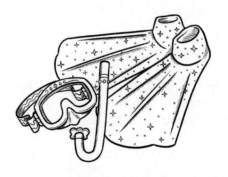

CHAPTER ONE

Water Fight

"Yum," said Charlotte Williams, helping herself to a still-warm orange and cranberry muffin. She and her family were having breakfast on their sunny patio.

Charlotte took a big bite of muffin. "These are delicious, Dad," she said.

"Thanks," said Dad. "I used the oranges from our trees."

Back in England, Charlotte's family had had apple trees in their garden. But here in California, where they had moved not long ago, there were orange trees in their yard. Dad was always thinking up new recipes to use up the fruit.

"What are we doing today?" asked Liam, Charlotte's little brother.

"Can we go to the beach?" said Harvey, Liam's twin.

Charlotte nodded eagerly, her mouth too full of muffin to speak.

"The surf conditions are supposed to be great today," said Dad.

"What about your homework?" said Mum, sipping freshly squeezed orange juice.

12

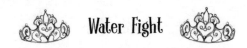

"We finished it yesterday after school," said Harvey.

"The beach sounds great," said Mum. "But we need to get all our weekend chores done first."

Liam and Harvey groaned as Mum pulled out a to-do list.

"What should we do first?" Charlotte asked helpfully. She knew that the sooner they got their chores done, the sooner they'd all be riding the waves!

Studying her list, Mum said, "I'll mow the lawn, your dad can vacuum, and you kids can wash the car."

After clearing the breakfast things away, Charlotte and her brothers went into the garage to fetch a bucket and three big sponges. Charlotte filled the bucket up with water from the hose and added special soap, sloshing it around to make the water bubbly.

Dipping their sponges in the sudsy water, Charlotte and her brothers soaped the car.

"You two should give yourselves a wash while you're at it," Charlotte teased. "You're beginning to pong." Her brothers hated taking a bath!

"You should talk – I can smell your cheesy feet all the way over here," Harvey said, tossing his sponge at Charlotte.

SPLAT! It hit her in the chest, soaking her T-shirt.

Playfully narrowing her brown eyes, Charlotte said, "That's it! You asked for it!" She grabbed the hose and chased Harvey around the car.

SQUIRT! Charlotte sprayed Harvey.

Rushing to his twin's defence, Liam chucked a soggy sponge at Charlotte, but it

missed – hitting Harvey on the back!

"Oi!" cried Harvey. He grabbed the hose away from Charlotte and sprayed Liam.

Shrieking with laughter, Charlotte and her brothers ran around the car, pelting each other with wet sponges and spraying each other with the hose. Soon they were

all soaking wet and covered in soapy suds –
but at least the car was clean!

"Time out!" gasped Charlotte, making a
T-shape with her hands. "We'd better finish
the car or we'll never get to the beach."

She and her brothers got to work drying
off the car with soft cloths.

"Good job," shouted Mum over the noise
of the lawnmower.

When the car was so clean it sparkled in
the sunshine, Charlotte and her brothers
ran into the house, leaving wet footprints
on the carpet.

"It looks like you've already been
swimming," Dad chuckled, tousling
Charlotte's damp brown curls. "Go and put

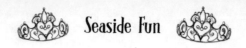

your swimming costumes on."

Upstairs, Charlotte changed into a sporty navy blue swimming costume. She picked up a joke book that had fallen on the floor and put it on her bedside table, next to a heart-shaped ceramic box.

Charlotte carefully touched the box, which had a mermaid painted on the lid. Her best friend, Mia Thompson, had made it and sent it to Charlotte all the way from England. Charlotte ran her finger over the mermaid's green hair and silvery tail. She looked exactly like their mermaid friend, Marina!

Charlotte and her best friend Mia had met Marina at Wishing Star Palace, a

magical place in the clouds where the girls were training to become Secret Princesses. Meeting mermaids was just one of the amazing things that had happened to them since they'd started their training. They got to go on wonderful adventures and use magic to grant people's wishes!

. Charlotte felt a stab of worry as she thought about Marina and their other mermaid friends. The mermaids had been forced to leave the beautiful Blue Lagoon and move into the palace swimming pool. Princess Poison, the Secret Princesses' enemy, had sent a frog named Toxin to poison their home, turning the lagoon's water slimy and green.

19

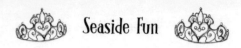

Princess Poison used to be a Secret Princess, but she had been banished from Wishing Star Palace for using wishes to gain more power. Now she used her bad magic to cause problems for the Secret Princesses – and their friends.

The only way to break Princess Poison's curse was to grant four watery wishes.

Don't worry, Charlotte told the mermaid on the heart-shaped box silently. *Mia and I are going to fix the lagoon. We won't let Princess Poison stop us.*

Charlotte glanced down at her wish necklace and gasped. Two beautiful aquamarines, which she and Mia had earned for granting two watery wishes,

glittered in the gold
half-heart pendant.
But the blue jewels
weren't what made
Charlotte gasp
– it was because
the necklace was
glowing!

Charlotte clasped her
pendant in her hand. "I wish I could see
Mia," she whispered. Light flooded out of
the pendant and swirled around Charlotte.
She shivered with excitement as she felt
herself being swept away from her bedroom.
Charlotte couldn't wait to see her best
friend! She knew her family wouldn't worry

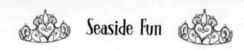

while she was away – thanks to the magic they wouldn't even notice she was gone.

A moment later, Charlotte found herself in a big, sunny kitchen filled with gleaming copper pans. Her swimming costume had magically transformed into a floaty pink princess dress. A girl in a pretty gold dress with a diamond tiara on her long blonde hair was waiting for her.

"Hi, Mia!" said Charlotte, running over to give her best friend a hug.

Mia's blue eyes shone happily as she hugged Charlotte back. "I was expecting the magic to take us to the swimming pool," she said. "I wonder why we've come to the palace kitchen instead?"

They didn't have to wait long to find
out. Two Secret Princesses burst into the
kitchen. Spotting the girls, Princess Sylvie,
who had red hair and a cupcake-shaped
pendant on her necklace, squealed, "Oh,
goodie! They're here!"

Princess Kiko, a gymnastics coach back in
the real world, tucked her sleek black bob

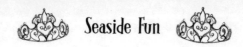

behind her ears. "We need your help, girls,"
she said. "We're going to make seaweed
sushi for the mermaids."

"But we don't know how to make sushi,"
said Mia.

"Then it's a good thing I can teach you!"
said Princess Kiko, grinning.

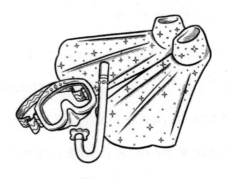

CHAPTER TWO
Sushi Surprise

"It would be faster to make the sushi using magic," said Sylvie. "But it's much more fun to make it by hand."

"What should we do first?" asked Mia.

They gathered around the table and Princess Kiko handed them each a mat made of thin bamboo strips.

"Why are the mats wet?" asked Charlotte.

"So the sushi doesn't stick to them as we're making it," explained Princess Kiko. She took out a packet of thin, green sheets. "Cover your mat with a layer of nori," she instructed them.

"What is this stuff?" asked Mia.

"Seaweed," said Sylvie.

"Ew," said Mia, wrinkling her nose.

"It's delicious!" Kiko assured her.

"Hey," said Charlotte. "Where does seaweed look for a job?"

Mia groaned – Charlotte loved bad jokes.

"The *kelp*-wanted ads," said Charlotte.

"Actually, that wasn't too bad," said Mia, grinning.

"I've got a new joke book," said Charlotte.

Next the girls spread sticky rice on top of the seaweed.

"Now add the veggies," said Sylvie.

Copying Kiko and Sylvie, Mia and Charlotte arranged a row of cucumber slices down the middle of their mats.

"This bit can be tricky," warned Kiko.

She showed the girls how to roll their mats up, pressing the ingredients into a sushi roll.

"Ta da!" said Mia proudly, showing off her sushi roll.

"Good work," said Sylvie, slicing the long sushi rolls into round pieces.

Next they made rainbow sushi, filled with carrot, pepper and beetroot, and avocado sprinkled with sesame seeds.

"How are the mermaids doing?" asked Mia as they worked.

"They're fine," said Sylvie. "Just really missing home."

"Let's go and see them," said Kiko. "I think we've made enough sushi."

They all clicked the heels of their sparkling ruby slippers three times and said, "The swimming pool."

Their magic shoes lifted them into the air. They flew over Wishing Star Palace, flags fluttering from its four white turrets, and landed by a spectacular crown-shaped swimming pool surrounded by palm trees. And best of all, mermaids swam in the clear turquoise water, their beautiful tails sparkling in the sunlight.

Across the pool, Princess Sophie had set

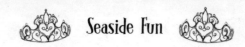

up her easel and was painting the portrait
of a young mermaid with a silver tail and
pale green hair. The mermaid was posing by
the side of the pool, but when she noticed
the girls she dived into the water and swam
over to greet them.

"I'm not done yet, Marina!" cried
Princess Sophie. Turning, she saw Mia and
Charlotte. "Oh, hi!" she said. "Now I know
why Marina was so excited."

"Sorry we interrupted your painting,
Sophie," said Mia.

"Don't worry," said Sophie, putting down
her paintbrush with a laugh. "I'll finish it
another time."

"Come and swim!" said Marina.

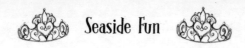

"Not now," said Kiko. "First we have a surprise for you."

"Yippee! I love surprises!" squealed Marina, slapping her tail against the water.

Princess Sylvie waved her wand and a low table appeared by the steps of the pool. The sushi feast they'd prepared in the kitchen was spread across the table.

"Ooh! This looks wonderful," said Oceane, swimming over to sit on the steps.

There were cushions on the opposite side of the table. Mia and Charlotte knelt down next to Sylvie, Kiko and Sophie.

"Mia and Charlotte helped make it," said Kiko, pouring out cups of green tea.

"I love sushi," said Coral, a mermaid with

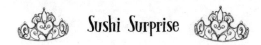

a purple tail and copper-coloured hair.

"Me too," said Nerida, a quiet mermaid
with dark hair and a turquoise tail.

A mermaid with a ruby-red tail swam up
to the steps. She pulled out an aquamarine
hair comb and strawberry-blonde hair
streaked with red tumbled down her back.
With a shimmer, her tail transformed into
legs and she climbed out of the pool.

"Hi, Alice," said Charlotte. She and Mia
knew Princess Alice best of all the Secret
Princesses, because Alice had been their
babysitter when they were little.

"Hi, girls," said Princess Alice, squeezing
in between them and setting her
aquamarine comb down on the table.

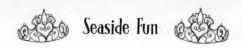

"You're so lucky," said Charlotte. "You can turn into a mermaid whenever you want."

"You'll earn your own aquamarine combs soon," said Alice. "Just one more watery wishes to go."

"Should we check the Magic Pearl now?" asked Mia. "Maybe someone's made a watery wish."

"First have some sushi," said Oceane. "After all, you helped make it."

"Does everyone know how to use chopsticks?" asked Kiko. She demonstrated the correct way to hold them.

"Dig in!" said Princess Sylvie, dunking a cucumber roll into a dish of soy sauce.

Charlotte picked up an avocado roll
with her chopsticks and popped it into her
mouth. It was delicious!

"Aren't you going to have some?" she
asked Mia.

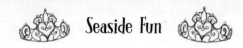

"I'm not sure I'll like it," admitted Mia.

"I wasn't sure about sushi either," said Alice. "But I tried it when I was on tour in Japan and now it's one of my favourite foods." Back in the real world, Alice was a pop star. She'd won a TV talent show and become a famous singer.

Mia bravely tasted a piece of rainbow sushi. "Mmm," she said. "It's really yummy."

She dipped another piece into some green paste and bit into it. "Whoa!" Mia fanned her hand in front of her mouth. "Too hot!"

Alice quickly waved her wand and Mia breathed a sigh of relief.

"That's better," she said gratefully, gulping down some green tea.

"Go easy on the wasabi next time," Alice said, grinning. "It's hot stuff."

When everyone had eaten their fill of sushi, Marina asked, "What's for dessert?"

"Oh my goodness!" cried Sylvie. "I completely forgot about pudding!"

"Don't worry," said Oceane. "We've had plenty."

"There's always room for dessert," insisted Princess Sylvie. She waved her wand and a gorgeous cake appeared on the table. It was decorated with white chocolate pearls, seashells made from icing sugar, and marzipan seahorses.

The chocolate pearls reminded Charlotte of the watery wish she and Mia needed to

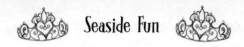

grant. "Let's go and check the Magic Pearl,"
she murmured to Mia.

The girls stood up. "We're going to try
and grant another wish," said Mia.

A chorus of "good lucks" rang out as the
girls clicked the heels of their ruby slippers
together three times and said, "The Magic
Pearl." The magic swept them to a coral
cave by the Blue Lagoon. Murky green
water lapped at the entrance.

"Ugh!" said Mia, looking at the lagoon in
dismay. "The water still stinks."

"Let's go and find out who we need to
help," said Charlotte, "so we can get out
of here!"

A beautiful pearl lit up the cave with

its soft, pink glow. The image of a girl
with cornrows finished with yellow beads
was reflected on the
pearl's shimmering
surface. Her
freckled face
looked
friendly, but
her brown
eyes were sad.

Mia and Charlotte
placed their hands on the pearl and a
message appeared:

Tanesha's made a wish
by the water so blue,

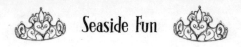

Say her name
to help make it come true!

"Tanesha!" the girls called out together.

Magical bubbles floated up, making the girls lighter than air and lifting them away from the palace. The girls landed by a little parade of shops on a sunny seafront. Their princess dresses had magically transformed into shorts and T-shirts.

Charlotte squinted in the sunshine, searching the beach for Tanesha. "I don't see her."

The girls wandered over to a shop selling beach toys, towels and souvenirs. A faded sign above it said *Beachcomber Gifts*.

Sushi Surprise

"We could do with a some of these," Mia
said, turning a spinner of sunhats.

SQUAWK! A seagull swooped down and
grabbed a sunhat in its beak.

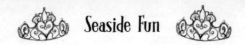

Suddenly the girl from the Magic Pearl burst out of the shop. "Hey! Stop it!" Tanesha shouted at the naughty seagull. "Give that hat back!"

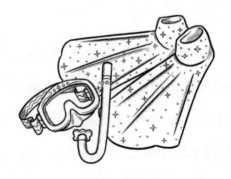

CHAPTER THREE
Seaside Souvenirs

Quick as a flash, Charlotte leapt into action and snatched the sunhat away from the seagull.

SQUAWK! The seagull flapped its wings and flew away.

"Thanks so much!" said Tanesha as Charlotte handed her the sunhat she'd rescued. "I'm Tanesha, by the way."

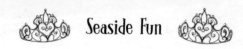

"No problem," said Charlotte, smiling. "I'm Charlotte and this is my friend, Mia."

Mia gave Tanesha a shy wave.

"We moved here a few weeks ago," said Tanesha. "I still can't get over how cheeky the seagulls are!"

"It's cool you get to live close to the sea," Mia said.

"Yeah, I can see it from my bedroom," said Tanesha, pointing to a window above the shop. "My parents run the shop. They decided to move here because they thought it would be better for me and my little sister, Jada. More fresh air and that sort of stuff." Tanesha didn't sound very enthusiastic.

"Don't you like it here?" Mia asked her curiously.

Tanesha shrugged. "It's OK. Well – apart from the seagulls. I just don't really fit in."

"Are the kids at school being mean?" Charlotte asked. She remembered how scary it had been when she first moved to California. Luckily, the kids at her new school had been really kind and she'd quickly made friends.

"Oh, everyone at school has been really nice," said Tanesha. "But they all spend all their free time at the beach."

"Don't you know how to swim?" Mia asked sympathetically.

"That's not it," said Tanesha. The beads on the ends of her cornrows rattled as she shook her head. "I'm a good swimmer, but I don't know how to surf or snorkel. Everyone at school is obsessed with water sports. A girl named Bea invited me to join them this afternoon but I don't know how." She sighed. "I really wish I could go surfing with them, but I don't want to look like an idiot."

Mia and Charlotte exchanged looks. Now

they understood why Tanesha seemed sad. Luckily, Charlotte was pretty sure they could help!

"I know how to surf," said Charlotte. "I could teach you."

"I don't know," said Tanesha hesitantly. "They'll all be really good at surfing. I'll make a fool of myself."

"No you won't. Charlotte's a really good teacher," said Mia. "She taught me how to surf!"

Charlotte smiled at her friend, remembering the fun they'd had when Mia had come to visit her in California.

"Well, if you're sure," said Tanesha. "There's some old surf stuff in our beach hut.

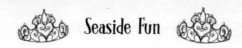

But I can't go until I finish my chores."

"We'll help," Mia offered quickly. "That way you'll get it done faster."

Charlotte grinned. "I'm glad I'm not the only one who has to do weekend chores."

Tanesha led them into the shop. It was crammed full of beach things – from boogie boards to buckets and spades, piled high on shelves from the floor to the ceiling.

"Taneeeeeesha!" shouted a chubby little girl with her black hair in two little buns. She launched herself at Tanesha's legs.

Tanesha picked up the toddler. "Hi, Jada," she said. "Meet Mia and Charlotte."

Jada waved at the girls.

A lady came out of the back room

carrying a clipboard. She had short, curly hair and a pencil tucked behind her ear. "Tanesha, love," she said. "Could you unpack the new deliveries?"

"Sure, Mum," said Tanesha. "My friends Mia and Charlotte are going to help."

"That's nice," said Tanesha's mum. "I'm going to take Jada for a walk before the shop gets busy. Dad worked late last night so he's having a lie-in."

As Jada and her mum set off, Tanesha and the girls got to work.

"Let's start by putting out the beach toys," suggested Tanesha. She opened a big cardboard box and the girls started unpacking the contents.

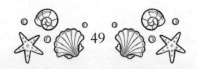

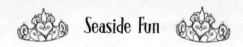

"Catch!" called Charlotte, tossing Mia a striped beach ball.

Mia caught the ball and added it to a metal bin full of bouncy balls. Tanesha hung colourful plastic spades on a rack, while Charlotte restocked a bin with fishing nets.

"Now we need to blow up the inflatables," said Tanesha.

Charlotte started puffing into a float shaped like a dolphin.

"It will take ages if we do it that way," said Tanesha, giggling. "We've got a special air pump."

"Phew!" panted Charlotte. "I'm out of puff already!"

Working as a team, they quickly blew
up inflatables shaped like crocodiles, car
tyres and doughnuts and hung them outside
the shop. Next, they refilled spinners with
sunglasses, flip-flops and
snorkels.

"What do you
think?" asked
Charlotte, trying
on a pair of heart-
shaped sunglasses
and striking a
glamorous pose.

"Fab," said Mia.

Glancing at the tide
that was beginning to

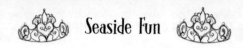
come in, Charlotte took off the sunglasses
and put them back on the rack. "We'd
better get back to work so we can hit the
waves."

"Let's do the postcards next," said
Tanesha, checking her mum's clipboard.
They restocked the rack with cheerful
scenes of white cliffs, lighthouses and fishing
boats.

"This will be you soon," Mia told
Tanesha, holding up a postcard of a surfer
riding a big wave.

"Hopefully," said Tanesha.

There was one more box to unpack, filled
with trinkets and souvenirs.

"Does this remind you of anyone?" Mia

whispered, showing Charlotte a magnet of a mermaid with copper hair and a glittery purple tail.

Charlotte nodded. It looked a lot like their mermaid friend, Coral!

The concern in Mia's blue eyes was mirrored in Charlotte's brown ones. They had to teach Tanesha how to surf. The mermaids back at the palace were counting on them to grant Tanesha's wish and break Princess Poison's spell!

"I think that's everything," said Tanesha, when they had finished hanging up a selection of keyrings shaped like anchors, sandcastles and seashells. "Thanks so much for your— Eeeek!"

Shrieking, Tanesha ran behind the shop's counter and hid.

"What's wrong?" asked Mia.

"A frog!" screamed Tanesha, pointing at the doorway.

Charlotte turned around and saw a big, ugly green frog squatting in the shop's entrance. Its eyes bulged menacingly as it puffed out its cheeks.

RIBBIT!

Toxin, Princess Poison's frog, hopped right into the shop.

It bounded on top of a spinner full of jewellery and sent it crashing to the floor. Toxin hopped over the spilled necklaces and bracelets, covering the jewellery in green slime. Croaking loudly, the frog leaped from shelf to shelf, leaving poisonous goo over the mugs and magnets, pencils and paperweights. Soon every souvenir in the shop was covered in slime. Then Toxin hopped up on the counter.

"Whatever you do, don't touch it!" warned Mia. "It's poisonous."

Tanesha cowered away from the frog, which sprang off the counter and hopped towards the stock room. "Help!" she whimpered, looking frightened.

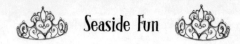

Charlotte looked at Mia and nodded. The two friends could help Tanesha. It was time to make a wish!

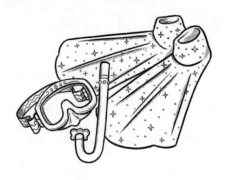

CHAPTER FOUR
Sand Surfing

Mia and Charlotte held their necklaces together, the pendants forming a perfect heart.

"I wish for the shop to be fixed," said Mia.

Magical golden light streamed out of the heart and transformed the shop. Now a jolly blue and white awning hung above the shop front. Nautical bunting, with red, white and

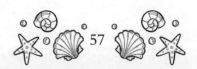

blue flags, stretched across the shop. A small wooden rowing boat had appeared in the middle of the shop, displaying an array of seaside gifts, toys and souvenirs. A mural of dolphins had been painted on the front of the counter. All the displays that Toxin had knocked over had been put right, and not a drop of green poison remained.

"Oh my gosh!" gasped Tanesha, staring round in astonishment. "The shop looks amazing! What did you just do?"

"Magic," Mia said simply.

"Huh?" said Tanesha.

"Mia and I are training to become Secret Princesses," explained Charlotte. "Our necklaces let us do magic. We came here to

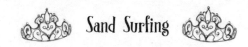

grant your wish."

For a moment, Tanesha stared at them in disbelief. Then a loud *RIBBIT* cut through the silence. Toxin hopped out of the back room, eyeing them maliciously.

"Uh-oh," said Charlotte. Their wish had cleaned up Toxin's mess, but it hadn't got rid of the frog!

Before she and Mia could figure out what to do about Toxin, Jada and her mum returned to the shop. Tanesha's little sister was licking a lollipop that she'd managed to get all over her face and hands.

"FROGGIEEEEE!" shrieked Jada excitedly. She ran towards the frog, her sticky hands outstretched.

"Oh no!" gasped Charlotte.

"Don't touch it!" cried Mia.

Tanesha darted forward and scooped her little sister up.

"But I want to play with the FROGGIEEEE!" screeched Jada, trying to break free.

Jada's noisy shrieks were too much for Toxin. The frog bounded out of the shop and Jada burst into tears.

"There, there," said Tanesha's mum, stroking Jada's back soothingly. "The froggie didn't want to play."

"Toxin's no match for a toddler temper tantrum," Charlotte murmured in Mia's ear.

"Thanks for your help," said Tanesha's

mum. She didn't mention how much the shop had changed. "You girls deserve a treat. Help yourself to an ice lolly from the shop freezer."

Tanesha gave her mother a puzzled look. "OK." She lifted the lid of the freezer, revealing a selection of frozen treats.

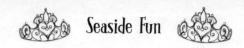

Mia helped herself to a strawberry lolly, Charlotte chose an ice cream covered in chocolate, and Tanesha took one shaped like a rocket.

"Thanks," said Mia and Charlotte as they licked their ice lollies.

"You can head down to the beach with your friends now, Tanesha," said her mum. "But make sure there's a lifeguard on duty if you go in the water."

"I'll just run upstairs and put my swimming costume on," said Tanesha, disappearing into the back room.

"Me come too!" wailed Jada.

"No, Jada," said Tanesha's mum. "You need a nap. But don't worry, we'll go down

to the beach later on."

Charlotte put the heart-shaped sunglasses
back on and made a funny face at Jada.
The little girl laughed, her tears forgotten.

Tanesha came back and the girls headed
down the beach, licking their ice lollies.
They passed a lifeguard in red swimming
trunks sitting in a tall chair and made their
way to a row of brightly painted beach huts.

"Why wasn't my mum surprised by how
different the shop looked?" Tanesha asked
the girls.

"That's just how the magic works,"
explained Charlotte. "Only the person
whose wish we're granting knows what
we're doing."

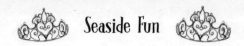

"Can you do that thing with your necklaces again so that I know how to surf?" asked Tanesha.

Mia shook her head. "Our magic isn't powerful enough for that," she said. "But we can grant three small wishes to help you."

Tanesha unlocked the door of a blue and white striped beach hut. It was painted white inside and flowery curtains hung at the windows. There was a tiny cooker, a little table and a day bed covered with a patchwork quilt.

"This is adorable," cooed Mia.

"It came with the shop," said Tanesha. "The old owner liked to surf and left some stuff behind."

Propped up against the back wall was a sun parasol, some snorkels, an old surfboard and some boogie boards.

Charlotte inspected the surfboard, which was a bit scuffed but otherwise fine. "We're in luck," she said. "The surfboard is about the right size for you, Tanesha."

Tanesha gulped nervously. "Isn't it a bit big?" she asked.

"It's easier to learn on a big board," Charlotte said.

Mia put her hand on Tanesha's shoulder. "Trust us. Charlotte knows what she's doing."

"OK," said Tanesha. "Let's do it." She picked up the surfboard and strode out of the beach hut.

Mia and Charlotte each grabbed a boogie board and hurried after her. Tanesha had nearly reached the water's edge.

"Not so fast!" called Charlotte. "We're going to start on the sand."

"On the sand?" asked Tanesha, confused.

"Yup," said Charlotte. "It's easier to practise on dry land first."

Mia nodded. "That's how I learned."

Tanesha set her surfboard down on the sand. Charlotte lay down on her tummy and showed Tanesha how to paddle her hands.

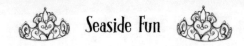

"This is how you get out into deeper water," said Charlotte.

Tanesha had a go, lying on her belly and paddling her arms as if she was in the water.

"Good," said Charlotte. "Now you need to learn how to pop up."

"Ooh, that's the tricky bit," said Mia.

Charlotte demonstrated how to do it a few times. She placed her palms flat on the surfboard and swiftly pushed her body up with her arms. In one fluid move, she tucked her knees underneath her so that she was crouching on the board. Then Charlotte stood up, her right foot forward and her left foot behind. "This is called goofy stance," she said.

The first time Tanesha attempted to pop up, she overbalanced and fell into the sand. "I definitely feel goofy now!" she laughed.

Charlotte smiled. "Goofy just means right foot forward. It's surfer slang. If you put

your left foot forward, that's called regular stance. Try it both ways – either one is fine."

Tanesha brushed the sand off and tried again. She managed to stay upright when she pushed herself up and jumped to her feet. This time her left foot was in front. "This feels better."

"Keep your knees bent and your arms loose," coached Charlotte.

Tanesha tried it again and again, until she could pop up smoothly.

"You're a quick learner," praised Mia. "It took me ages to get the hang of it."

"It's hard, though," said Tanesha. "My feet keep slipping."

"I know what will help," said Charlotte. "Wax. I bet there's some in the beach hut."

Leaving the surfboard and boogie boards on the sand, the girls ran back over to the beach hut.

"Found some!" called Charlotte, taking a bar of surf wax down off a shelf.

As they made their way back down the beach, Tanesha pointed and cried, "Hey! What's that guy doing?"

A short, tubby

man was stamping on the surfboard!

"Stop that!" cried Mia, running forward.

When they got closer, Charlotte saw who it was. "Cut it out, Hex!" she shouted at Princess Poison's assistant.

Grinning, Hex ignored her and jumped on the surfboard again.

SNAP! Tanesha's surfboard split in two!

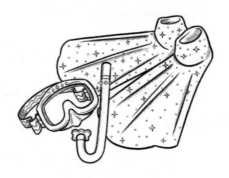

CHAPTER FIVE
Surf's Up!

"Oh no!" gasped Tanesha in dismay. "How am I going to learn how to surf now?"

"Oops!" said Hex. "I didn't think the surfboard belonged to anybody."

"Yes, you did," Charlotte accused him.

Mia glared at Hex, hands on her hips. "You knew exactly what you were doing."

"I was just looking for wood to make a

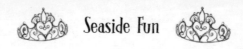
bonfire," said Hex. "So I can watch your
chances of granting a wish go up in flames!"
He cackled loudly.

BREEEEET! The lifeguard blew his whistle and hopped down from his tall wooden chair. He strode across the sand to them. "Is this man bothering you?" he asked the girls.

"Yes!" said Charlotte.

"Sir, I'm going to have to ask you to move along," the lifeguard said sternly.

"Don't worry – I was just leaving," said Hex. He stomped on the boogie boards as he went. *CRACK! CRUNCH!*

"Not the boogie boards too!" wailed Tanesha.

"Don't worry," Charlotte told her when the lifeguard had returned to his chair. "We've got this under control."

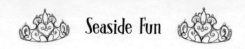

"Do you know that mean guy?" asked Tanesha.

"Unfortunately we do," said Mia, sighing. "His name is Hex. He works for someone called Princess Poison."

"Poison?" said Tanesha. "Does she have anything to do with that frog?"

"That was her frog," confirmed Mia. "Princess Poison and her helpers try to spoil wishes instead of granting them."

"They're doing a pretty good job of it," said Tanesha, staring down at the broken surfboard glumly.

"Cheer up," said Charlotte confidently. "We've never let them stop us before and we're not about to start now." Turning to

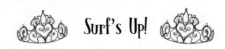

Mia, she said, "I think it's time to make another wish."

The girls held their pendants together. "I wish for Tanesha to have a new surfboard," said Charlotte.

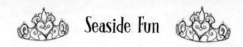

Golden light as bright as sunshine flared out of their necklaces. The broken surfboard vanished. In its place was a brand-new, hot pink surfboard. It had a colourful design of tropical flowers printed on it. Next to it, two new boogie boards with mermaids on them rested on the sand.

"Oh my gosh," said Tanesha.

"You look like a real surfer girl now," said Mia.

Tanesha looked down and gasped in surprise. Her bathing suit had magically been transformed into a hot pink wetsuit with the same flowery design as her surfboard. Mia and Charlotte's clothes had changed too. Now they were both wearing

Surf's Up!

swim shorts and co-ordinating long-sleeved
swim tops.

"I'll show you how to catch a wave, then
you can try," said Charlotte.

79

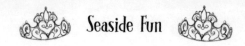

"If you think I'm ready," said Tanesha
nervously.

"First you need to attach your leash,"
said Charlotte, strapping a cuff around her
ankle. It was attached to the surfboard by
a cord. "If you fall off, the leash means you
won't get separated from your surfboard.
You can get it back easily."

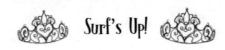

They all waded into the water, Tanesha and Mia holding boogie boards.

"Ooh!" gasped Mia when the waves reached her tummy. "It's a bit chilly!"

"Not for me," said Tanesha, grinning. "I've got a wetsuit!"

"Remember," said Charlotte as they went in deeper. "You should never paddle out

further than you can swim."

Charlotte paddled out a bit further, then turned her surfboard around so it was pointing inland. She straddled the end of her surfboard, waiting for the perfect wave. "Here comes a good one!" she cried.

Dropping down to her belly, Charlotte paddled furiously. Just before the wave broke, she popped up and stood on the board.

"Cowabunga!" whooped

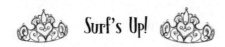

Charlotte, riding the wave into shore.

"That's what surfers shout when they're happy," Mia explained to Tanesha.

In shallow water, Charlotte jumped off the surfboard and took off the leash. "Your turn," she said, passing the surfboard to Tanesha.

Tanesha attached the cuff to her ankle.

"Oh! I almost forgot!" said Charlotte. "If there are other surfers in the water, whoever's closest to the top of the wave gets to ride it. Cutting across other surfers is rude – and dangerous too!"

Tanesha paddled further out then sat up on her surfboard. Wave after wave passed by, but Tanesha held back.

Mia and Charlotte paddled out on the boogie boards.

"What's up?" Charlotte asked Tanesha.

"I'm scared," confessed Tanesha. "I might fall off."

"So what?" said Mia. "Nobody's watching except us. And it's really fun if you do manage to stay on."

"You've got to just go for it," urged Charlotte. "Otherwise you'll never learn." She pointed out to sea. "Look! Here comes a good wave now."

Tanesha took a deep breath. She paddled out to catch the wave, but she was too slow. The wave crashed before she could get to her feet, knocking her off the board.

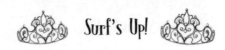

"Now I get why you need a leash," spluttered Tanesha, clambering back on to her surfboard.

"That was a good try," said Charlotte. "You just need to get up a bit faster."

Tanesha tried again. This time she managed to get to her feet, but lost her balance when the board shot forward.

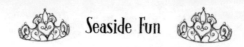

"I stink at this," Tanesha grumbled, heaving herself back on the surfboard.

"Don't be discouraged," said Mia. "You just need to stick at it."

"Even the best surfers fall off all the time," Charlotte assured Tanesha.

Tanesha's fixed her brown eyes on a big wave in the distance. "OK, here goes," she said, sounding determined. She paddled towards the wave and scrambled to her feet at just the right moment.

Her knees bent and her arms outstretched for balance, Tanesha glided over the frothy white wave. A huge smile spread across her face as she rode the wave to the shore.

"Yay!" cheered Mia and Charlotte,

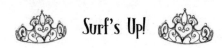

paddling in on their boogie boards.

"That was amazing!" said Tanesha, jumping off her surfboard.

"Told you so," said Mia, beaming at her.

"Way to go!" said Charlotte, giving Tanesha a high five.

VRRROOOM! The roar of a beach buggy's engine cut into their celebrations. The driver's long, jet-black hair blew back in the sea breeze as she raced along the sand. The buggy skidded to a stop at the water's edge, its wide tyres spraying sand all over the girls.

"Oh no," groaned Charlotte. The buggy's driver was the very last person she wanted to see – Princess Poison!

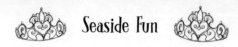

Pushing a single lock of white hair out of her face, Princess Poison climbed down from the buggy wearing a dark green wetsuit. "You girls seem very overexcited," she said, glowering at them. "I think it's time you calmed down."

Her green eyes glinted hatefully as she raised her wand. "Yes, it's time to calm EVERYTHING down – even the waves!"

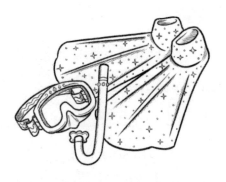

CHAPTER SIX

Making Waves

Princess Poison pointed her wand at the sea and hissed a spell:

**Turn the tide from high to low,
To deal the girls a nasty blow!**

Green light flashed out of the wand and instantly the sea was as smooth as glass.

Instead of big swells, gentle ripples lapped against the sand.

"How can we surf if there aren't any waves?" asked Tanesha.

"You can't," said Princess Poison triumphantly. "That's the whole point." She smirked at Mia and Charlotte as she climbed back into the beach buggy. "Looks like the tide has turned against you." With a harsh bark of laughter, Princess Poison zoomed off.

"Can you guess who that was?" Mia asked Tanesha.

"Um, does she have an ugly poisonous frog?" asked Tanesha.

"Got it in one," said Mia. "I'm afraid that

90

was Princess Poison."

Charlotte glanced down at her necklace. The pendant was glowing very faintly now, because nearly all its magic had been used up. "Let's sort this out," she said, pressing her pendant against Mia's.

"I wish for it to be high tide again," said Mia.

The last of the magical light shot out of the heart, and sparkles danced across the water. A huge wave crashed against the sand, covering their feet with white foam. The tide had turned once more!

"Thanks," said Tanesha. "I still have a little time before my friends arrive. I should probably keep practising."

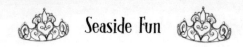

As Tanesha practised surfing, Mia and Charlotte played on their boogie boards. They paddled out on their tummies and then – *SWOOSH!* – let the waves carry them back to the beach.

"This is so fun," Mai said. "It's almost as good as having a mermaid tail."

"I know," agreed Charlotte. "But I can't wait to earn our combs." It wasn't just because becoming a mermaid was amazing – if they earned two more aquamarines they'd have broken Princess Poison's horrid curse, too!

Mia and Charlotte floated on their boogie boards watching Tanesha surf. She didn't always manage to stay on her surfboard, but

falling off didn't stop her from getting right back on and trying again.

"She's getting better and better," Charlotte said as Tanesha attempted her biggest wave yet. Tanesha wobbled a bit as she got to her feet, but she didn't fall off.

"Awesome!" Mia called.

Charlotte gave an admiring whistle as Tanesha glided on the wave.

"Yay, Tanesha!" came a high voice from behind them.

Charlotte turned and saw Jada clapping her chubby little hands. Next to her stood Tanesha's mum, smiling proudly. She held a bag in one hand and gave Tanesha a thumbs-up with the other hand.

The girls waded out of the water with their boards to join Tanesha's mum on the sand.

"Wow!" said Tanesha's mum. "I'm so impressed. You know how to surf!"

"Charlotte's a great teacher," Tanesha said modestly.

"And you're a really quick learner," said Mia. "You picked up surfing much faster than I did."

"Something smells good," said Tanesha, sniffing the air.

"It's fish and chips!" squealed Jada, jumping up and down.

"I thought you girls might be ready for lunch," said Tanesha's mum.

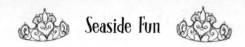

Charlotte's tummy rumbled as Tanesha's mum spread a picnic blanket on the sand and took several portions of fish and chips wrapped in newspaper out of her bag.

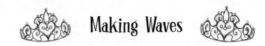

"Tuck in, girls, there's enough for everyone," said Tanesha's mum, opening a warm parcel and passing out cans of lemonade.

Her mouth watering, Charlotte unwrapped the paper, revealing crispy battered fish and fat, golden chips. "Yum!" she said, popping a chip in her mouth. It had been ages since she'd had British fish and chips – she'd forgotten how delicious it was!

"Thanks very much," said Mia politely.

"No, thank you," said Tanesha's mum. "You girls have put a smile back on Tanesha's face."

A seagull waddled across the sand and

stole one of Mia's chips.

"Hey!" she cried, shooing the pesky bird away.

"Naughty seagull!" shouted Jada. Flapping her little arms like wings, the toddler chased the seagull down the beach. It flew away, squawking.

Charlotte chuckled. "It's not just frogs that are scared of Jada – it's seagulls too."

"She's a menace," agreed Tanesha as Jada toddled back and plonked herself down on the blanket.

"What time are you meeting your friends?" Tanesha's mum asked.

"Two o'clock," said Tanesha. Suddenly she looked nervous. "I'll probably be rubbish

compared to the
other kids from
school." She
looked down,
fiddling with
the fringe of the
picnic blanket
anxiously. "Maybe I
shouldn't bother turning up ..."

"Hey," said Tanesha's mum, lifting up
Tanesha's chin. "What kind of talk is that?
My girl's not a quitter."

"You're doing great," Mia assured
Tanesha.

"Everyone was a beginner once,"
Charlotte reminded her.

"But what if I fall off in front of all the other kids?" worried Tanesha.

"Sometimes in life you need to take risks," said Tanesha's mum. "Moving to the seaside was a big risk for me and Dad. But if you don't try things, you'll miss out."

"Tanesha," said Jada, tugging on her sister's arm. "Take me into the water."

Holding her little sister's hand, Tanesha led Jada down to the water. Mia and Charlotte came along, too. As a wave washed up on the sand, Jada ran away, shrieking in fright.

"Aw," said Mia. "Don't be scared, Jada. The waves won't hurt you."

Charlotte giggled. "She's not afraid of

frogs or seagulls, but I guess waves are pretty scary when you're only little."

"Come on, Jada," coaxed Tanesha. "You've got to be brave."

Jada clutched Tanesha's hand and waded into the cold water. She squealed with shock and delight as water washed over her toes. Soon, she was splashing happily in the water with the older girls.

Mia and Charlotte each held one of Jada's hands. "One … two … three … WHEE!" they cried, swinging the laughing toddler high up into the air as another big wave rolled in.

"Time to go back to the shop," called Tanesha's mum as she folded up the picnic

blanket. "Are you going to stay to meet your friends?" she asked Tanesha.

Tanesha nodded. "If Jada can be brave, so can I."

"That's my girl," said Mum, planting a kiss on her daughter's forehead. "Have fun."

Not long after Jada and her mum left, a girl with a long ginger plait ran down the beach, holding a bright blue surfboard under her arm.

"Hi, Tanesha!" she said warmly. "I'm so glad you came."

"Hi, Bea," said Tanesha shyly. "These are my friends – Mia and Charlotte."

"Cool surfboard," said Bea, nodding at Tanesha's flowery surfboard.

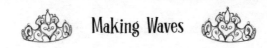

"It's new," said Tanesha. "I've just started to learn how to surf."

"That's OK," said Bea. "You'll get loads of practice now that you live here. We're always out in the sea, even when it's cold! It's so much fun!"

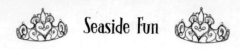
Several other boys and girls from
Tanesha's class joined, all wearing wetsuits
and holding snorkels and surfboards.

"Yo, dudes," said a boy with floppy blond
hair. "Those waves look epic."

"What are we waiting for?" asked Bea.
She ran into the water and paddled out
on her surfboard. A moment later she
caught the crest of a wave and rode it in.

"Cowabunga!" she hollered joyfully.

Tanesha hung back. "I'm scared. Bea's really good."

"Remember what you told Jada," Charlotte said. "Be brave."

"We'll come in with you," said Mia.

Tanesha paddled out on her surfboard, with Mia and Charlotte following behind on the boogie boards. As her classmates surfed, Tanesha sat up on her board watching them.

"Come on, Tanesha," called the blond boy as he surfed past. "Don't be a scaredy cat!"

"Don't be afraid to take a risk," said Charlotte.

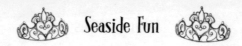

"You can do it," said Mia.

"OK," said Tanesha bravely. "Wish me luck." And, dropping to her tummy, she paddled her surfboard towards a big wave!

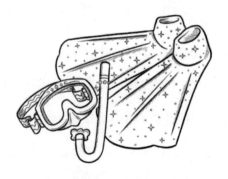

CHAPTER SEVEN
Total Wipeout

Tanesha caught the wave at its peak. As Charlotte and Mia watched with bated breath, Tanesha pushed herself up. She sprang to her feet smoothly.

"This is looking good," said Mia.

With her arms outstretched and a look of pure concentration on her face, Tanesha rode the wave.

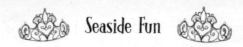

Suddenly, out of nowhere, a surfer in a
dark green wetsuit shot through the water.
She cut right in front of Tanesha.

"Is that—" said Mia.

"Princess Poison," said Charlotte, nodding
in concern.

Tanesha wobbled and flailed her arms as she struggled to stay upright. It was no use – the surfboard shot out from under her.

SPLASH! Tanesha fell into the water.

"Tanesha!" cried Mia. She and Charlotte gripped their boogie boards and kicked their legs, propelling themselves towards Tanesha.

Coughing, Tanesha bobbed to the surface. Mia pushed the stray surfboard closer to Tanesha, who hauled herself back on, coughing and spluttering.

"Are you OK?" Charlotte asked.

"I'm fine," said Tanesha. "Just embarrassed."

"You shouldn't be," said Mia. "It wasn't

your fault at all."

Tanesha headed back to the beach to catch her breath. Princess Poison was waiting for them.

"That was quite a wipeout," she gloated. "You've made rather a splash with your new friends."

"You haven't won," said Charlotte defiantly. "You won't stop us from granting Tanesha's wish."

"Oh, really?" said Princess Poison, arching her eyebrow. "How are you planning to do that now that your silly little necklaces have run out of magic?"

Bea hurried out of the water, holding her surfboard, and joined the girls. "That was

really uncool," she told Princess Poison. "Tanesha was riding that wave."

"Don't blame me," Princess Poison sniffed dismissively. "She fell off because she's rubbish at surfing."

"Dude," said the blond boy. "It's dangerous to cut someone up like that."

"I'll tell you what's dangerous," spat Princess Poison, her eyes flashing. "Messing with me!"

SQUAWK! A seagull swooped overhead. White bird poop plopped on top of Princess Poison's head. *SPLAT!*

"Gah!" she screamed.

"That seagull wasn't afraid to mess with you – or rather, ON you," said Charlotte.

Bea, the blond boy and the rest of Tanesha's classmates giggled.

Fuming, Princess Poison stormed off down the beach.

"It's meant to be good luck," Mia called after her. Her eyes twinkling mischievously, she added, "Good luck for us, that is!"

"Come on," said Bea, putting her arm around Tanesha's shoulder. "Let's get back out there."

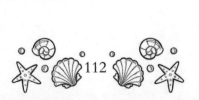

"I don't know …" said Tanesha.

"Don't bail on us," said the blond boy.

"Everyone wipes out sometimes."

All of the other kids nodded.

"The only reason you fell off was because that mean lady got in your way," said Bea.

Tanesha picked up her surfboard and followed her classmates into the water. As Mia and Charlotte watched from the beach, the surfers paddled out. This time, Tanesha didn't hesitate. As soon as she spotted a wave swelling in the distance, she paddled towards it. She got to her feet just in time and proudly rode it in.

"Cowabunga!" Tanesha shouted.

"Yippee!" cried Mia, jumping up and down excitedly.

"Hurrah!" cheered Charlotte.

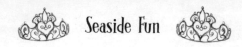

Beaming, Tanesha hopped off her surfboard. Bea and the blond boy paddled over to congratulate her. Mia and Charlotte waded into the water to hug Tanesha.

"That was great," said the blond boy.

"It was sick!" agreed Bea.

Tanesha grinned in delight.

"We're going to get ice creams," said Bea. "Want to come?"

"Um, I'll join you in a minute," said Tanesha.

As her friends headed to the snack bar, Tanesha smiled at Mia and Charlotte.

"You look stoked," said Charlotte.

"Does that mean really happy?" asked Tanesha. "Because that's how I feel. You

taught me how to surf, so now I can hang out with the other kids from school. Thank you for making my wish come true."

Cries of "Epic!" and "Awesome!" made the girls look out to sea.

Fountains of water shot into the air, along the whole length of the beach. Changing colour as they sprayed in perfect time with each other, the jets of water rose and fell, swirled and twirled, putting on a beautiful display. It was like watching a water ballet.

Mia and Charlotte grinned at each other. They knew the magical water show was because they had granted Tanesha's wish!

Suddenly, an enormous wave rose up. A surfer in an aquamarine-coloured wetsuit

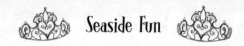

shot into it, riding through the hollow part
of the curl.

"OMG," said Charlotte. "That's called
tube riding. It's the ultimate surf trick. I've
never actually seen anyone do it before."

When she emerged from the tunnel of water, the surfer did another trick. She launched herself off another big wave and flipped up into the air. She somersaulted, grabbed her surfboard and landed neatly back on the board.

Everyone on the beach clapped and cheered.

As the surfer rode into shore, Charlotte realised who it was.

"It's Kiko!" said Charlotte.

Princess Kiko hopped off her surfboard, picked it up and waded out of the water to join them.

"Guess what that last trick was called?" asked Princess Kiko. "A sushi roll!"

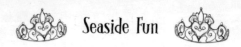

"How did you learn how to do that?" Tanesha asked Kiko.

"A lot of practice," said Kiko, winking.

"We've got to go now," Charlotte told Tanesha.

Tanesha hugged the girls. "Thank you so much," she told them. "I'll think of you every time I go surfing."

"Hopefully you'll be thinking of us a lot, then," said Mia, smiling.

As Tanesha joined her friends at the snack bar, Kiko said, "Great work, girls. You totally deserve your third aquamarines." She took out her wand and touched it first to Mia's necklace, and then to Charlotte's. Now there were three blue jewels sparkling

on their half-heart pendants.

"Only one more watery wish to grant," Charlotte said.

Mia squeezed her hand. "Then the mermaids will be able to go back home!"

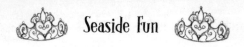

Princess Kiko smiled at them. "Right now it's time for the two of you to go home."

Mia and Charlotte hugged each other goodbye, then Kiko waved her wand again. Magic sent them spinning away from the beach.

Seconds later, Charlotte was back in her bedroom. She glanced down at the mermaid on the trinket box Mia had painted for her. *You'll be home soon*, she promised the mermaid. Suddenly, her brothers appeared in the doorway.

"Are you ready for the beach?" asked Harvey.

"Nearly!" said Charlotte. She grabbed her sunglasses and a sunhat and ran out of her

room. "Let's go!" Even though she'd only just got back, Charlotte couldn't wait to hit the beach again!

The End

Join Charlotte and Mia in their next
Secret Princesses adventure,

Tropical Party

read on for a sneak peek!

"You look gorgeous, Mum!" said Mia
Thompson.

Mia's mum was sitting at her dressing
table putting on glossy red lipstick, while
Mia and her little sister, Elsie, perched
on her bed watching her get ready for an
evening out with friends.

"You smell good too," said Elsie, sniffing

the air as Mum dabbed perfume behind her ears. "Like flowers."

Smiling, Mum turned around and squirted a bit of perfume on the girls. Then she twisted her hair, which was blonde like Mia's, into an elegant bun. As she looked at her reflection in the mirror, Mum frowned. "Hmm. Something's missing," she said.

"How about this?" suggested Mia, going over to the dresser and getting a beaded necklace.

As Elsie clomped around the bedroom in Mum's high heels, Mia fastened the necklace around her mum's neck. It sparkled against her new black dress.

"Perfect!" said Mia.

"It's not as pretty as yours," Mum tapped the gold half-heart necklace that Mia always wore and winked.

DING DONG! The doorbell rang.

"Gran's here!" shouted Elsie, kicking off Mum's shoes and charging downstairs to answer the door.

Mia followed Elsie downstairs and gave her grandmother a big hug, breathing in Gran's comforting scent. "Hi, Gran," she said happily.

Mum clattered downstairs in her high heels. "Be good for Gran," she told the girls.

"We will," promised Mia.

"Don't stay up too late," said Mum, grabbing her clutch bag.

"We won't," said Elsie.

Mum kissed them both goodbye, leaving lipstick marks on their cheeks.

"Have fun," called Gran, as Mum hurried out, shutting the door behind her.

"Now come and play, Gran!" said Elsie, tugging her grandmother's hand.

"I think I need a cup of tea first, Elsie," said Gran, laughing.

As she waited for the kettle to boil, Gran set her bag down on the kitchen counter and started singing. "Oooh! I'm gonna be a star," she crooned, pretending a spoon was a microphone.

Read Tropical Party to find out what happens next!

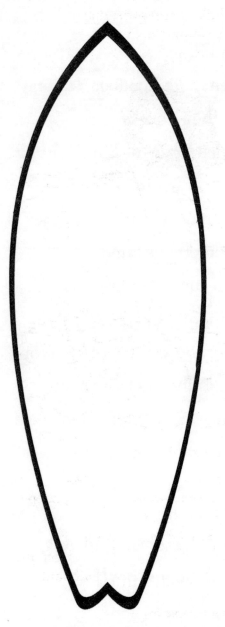

Surfboard Bookmark

Surfboards aren't just sports equipment – they are also works of art. From zigzags and zebra stripes to flowers, fruit and flames, surfboards come decorated with all sorts of eye-catching designs. What does your dream surfboard look like?

1. Use tracing paper to trace over the template.

2. Draw around your template on a sturdy piece of card.

3. Cut out the surfboard shape.

4. Now decorate your bookmark any way you like!

Surf Slang

Want to sound like a real surfer dude?
You need to know the lingo!

Amped
excited

Bail
to jump off your
surfboard

Baggies
loose surfing shorts

Barney
a beginner surfer

Chowder
dirty seawater

Cowabunga
what surfers shout
when riding a
wave

Epic
a word to describe
REALLY good
waves

Gnarly
dangerous surf
conditions

Paddlepuss
someone who stays
close to the shore,
away from the big
waves

Sick
a compliment for a
cool surfing move

Stoked
really happy

Wipe out
to fall off your
surfboard

Secret
PRINCESSES

What would you wish for?

Are you a Secret Princess?

Join the Secret Princesses Club at:

secretprincessesbooks.co.uk

Explore the magic of the
Secret Princesses and discover:

♥ Special competitions! ♥
♥ Exclusive content! ♥
♥ All the latest princess news! ♥